THE DOLL

By:
Ava Jamaleddin

To: My teachers, my family, and others who helped me through this work

CONTENTS

Chapter 1
"SNACK TIME"

"MOM! I found the one I want!" yelled Jenna.

"Which one is it, honey?" asked Mom with a happy expression.

Jenna looked at her mom and said, "This one..."

Mom smiled at Jenna and said, "Okay, honey, anything for you. Is that all you want?"

"Yes, Mom," Jenna replied happily.

The doll had short, orange hair and pale brown and green eyes. She was wearing a fluffy, dark blue dress. However, the doll made the mother uncomfortable for some reason.

Once home, Jenna exclaimed, "YAY! WO-HOOOOO! I love her, thank you Mom!"

Mom looked at her smiling face and said warmly, "Love you, honey. Good night."

When Jenna got dressed for bed, she realized that she was still hungry. However, Jenna had a fear of being alone, so she took her doll with her. Once she got downstairs, she noticed that her mom was sleeping on the couch. Then she noticed a creak every time she took a step.

Soon, her mother woke up and asked, "What are you doing up at this time of night?"

Jenna panicked and whispered nervously, "I'm hungry, Mom, so I just came down for a snack. Are you mad at me?"

Her mother replied by saying, "Well if you're *that* hungry you may fetch a snack. But be quick and quiet; your dad is sleeping."

Jenna looked at her and said, "Okay, Mom."

Jenna grabbed her snack, quickly ate it, and tiptoed back upstairs. Her mom smiled and giggled as she heard the creaks from the staircase.

When Jenna went to bed she dreamed of being in a candy castle, wearing a light blue, shiny dress. She then walked into the castle, grabbed a big cookie,

Ava & Melody Production, LLC.

and took a huge bite. She looked around and saw a pillow made from a huge marshmallow, clouds made of cotton candy, and blankets made of Fruit Roll-Ups. Then, in her mind, she said, "What a beautiful world."

She smiled as she walked along, noticing a small village of houses made entirely of gingerbread.

But suddenly she woke up to the sound of loud screams coming from her window. Scared, she barely glanced out before she ran to her parents' room, jumped on their bed, and huddled between her mother and father. She didn't say a word, but she *did* notice that the screams had been from children. The last thing she remembered from peeking out of her window had been the sight of her doll holding a knife.

Chapter 2
"TIME FOR SCHOOL"

"Morning, Mom," Jenna said in a tired voice and her mother returned the greeting.

"Honey, breakfast is ready," her dad chimed in.

"Yay! What are we eating today?" asked Jenna, perking up a little.

"Pancakes, waffles, toast and butter, hard-boiled eggs, a doughnut, cereal, and some oatmeal left from yesterday," replied her father.

"Yum," said Jenna.

As they sat at the table, they held hands and prayed as usual, then made one wish. Jenna wished to live a

Ava & Melody Production, LLC.

peaceful life. Her father wished for a new computer because his was broken. Jenna's mother wished for Jenna to have a great day at school. After they prayed and wished, they gobbled up their food. By the time they were set to leave for school, the table was empty – nothing but cups, plates, and used napkins.

It was time for Jenna to start her first day at middle school. Jenna was a little scared, since she'd heard that people were often bullied in middle school. However, her mother told her to be brave no matter what happens. Her words put a glowing smile on Jenna's face and she rushed to the school bus.

Once she got on the school bus, she saw multiple kids were already sitting there. The seats had small holes on them, some a little bigger. The bus smelled like a rubber band that had just been unpackaged. Jenna thankfully made some friends on the bus. Once she got to school and looked in her backpack, she was surprised to see that her doll was inside. For a wild moment Jenna thought the doll was possessed, but she reasoned her mom had just put it inside.

Her first period was science, which was her least favorite subject. She learned about the chemicals in sea water and a lot more. Jenna's second period was math, which was her favorite subject. In math class she learned decimals and how you multiply them. Her last subject was social studies, which she also loved. In social studies she learned about "John C. Fermont," a famous person.

At lunch there were hot dogs, burgers and fries, and mac 'n' cheese. There were also sides of carrots, apples, and broccoli. Jenna sat with her new friends, called Sarah and Emma. They were very nice. Jenna was talking about her birthday the next day nonstop and she invited five people to her party – Emma, Sarah, Logan, Andrew, and a shy girl called Chloe.

They were all excited about the party. Jenna said that there were going to be two flavored cakes, one chocolate and one vanilla. The goody bags all had one Pop-It, a random key chain, and one Starbucks drink sticker. Jenna had made twenty-two goody bags for some reason.

Jenna ate all her food and packed her backpack. She put her three books – math, social studies, and science – in her backpack but soon noticed that her doll was gone. She got worried, so she called her mom to check whether she'd been imagining things – had the doll really been in her bag earlier? Her Mom said that her doll was on her bed.

Jenna sighed with relief to know her doll was safe and boarded the school bus.

Ava & Melody Production, LLC.

Chapter 3
"THE PARTY"

At home, Jenna rushed to do her homework quickly and finished it within one hour. She was filled with happiness because her party was the very next day. She got all the party decorations ready in less than two hours. Soon after that, it was her bedtime at 9:30 pm. Jenna said her parents goodnight and left for bed.

The next morning, Jenna got ready in less than a minute. She ran downstairs so quickly that it sounded like a stampede. Jenna hugged her parents, ate her breakfast, and left for school. At school, every 6th grader cheered and yelled happy birthday for her. Jenna smiled as everyone hugged her.

That afternoon, Jenna got off the school bus and rushed into the house. She yelled, "THEY'LL BE HERE ANY MINUTE!!!"

Her dad walked up to her and said, "Calm down, beautiful, the house is ready."

Five minutes later, Jenna heard the bell ring. Jenna then yelled, "THEY'RE HERE, DAD, THEY'RE HERE!"

Jenna ran to the door and opened it to see Chloe, Sarah, Emma, Logan, and Andrew all smiling at her. Jenna gave them a big, juicy hug and quickly grabbed the gifts, then gave them to her mother.

They ran upstairs to see the creepy doll.

Chloe said in a terrified voice, "Jenna, what is that? Is that your doll?"

Jenna replied promptly, saying, "Yeah. Why, Chloe?"

They all stared at her in horror and asked, "Can we leave your room...? NOW!"

Jenna took them out of the room and asked, concerned, "Why?"

Andrew said, "Because that doll was seen in the middle of the street a few days ago, stabbing my little brother!!! He's in the hospital!"

Jenna looked at him in disbelief. "What? Why would I ever believe you..." she asked, then paused as a memory returned to her. "Wait. My doll is creepy... I- I saw her stabbing a little kid, too."

Ava & Melody Production, LLC.

Jenna then let out a huge, horrified scream. Her parents barely heard her because she had told them to put on loud music, but her mom heard enough of a small scream to run upstairs and see what was going on.

What she saw horrified her. The doll was standing in Jenna's room, holding a knife, and repeating, "Kill, kill, kill, kill, kill."

Jenna's mom immediately passed out from sheer terror. When Jenna realized her mom had passed out and fallen near the doll, Jenna started to cry and start to yell for her dad.

Her dad ran upstairs so quickly that the steps didn't even have the chance to creak. Her dad was so shocked by the sight that he almost passed out too. Jenna could hear the doll still repeating "kill," but it seemed her dad couldn't for some reason. The terror grew so much that, for a moment, Jenna thought she might even pass out like her mother.

Later, at the hospital, Jenna's mom made a quick and easy recovery. Jenna ran to her mom once she entered the room and gave her the tightest hug. It was so tight that her mom could barely speak.

Jenna gave a big smile, then got quiet. After about 30 second of staring at each other, Jenna's father walked into the room too. He was half smiling, half nervous. Jenna immediately knew something was wrong. So, Jenna walked to her father and whispered, "Why so down?"

Her father replied, "...Throw that doll away."

Ava & Melody Production, LLC.

Chapter 4
"THE ROAD TRIP"

A few days later they left on a road trip to San Francisco. Jenna made a list of all the supplies she needed: swimsuit, three pairs of pajamas, three T-shirts, running shoes, slippers, socks, pants, a beach hat, a phone, a sketch pad, and the doll.

Jenna also brought a small bag of snacks, like gummies, two peanut butter and jelly sandwiches, water, three cheese sticks, and some carrots.

Her mother packed some pants, hats, shirts, money, and her phone, but no warmer clothes because she knew that San Francisco was hot. Jenna's father packed jeans, a buttoned shirt, some nice shoes, and his phone and wallet.

Jenna's parents shared a suitcase while she had a smaller one of her own. When they got into the car,

Jenna's dad turned on the radio straight away. They listened to some classical music, jazz, and rock. Jenna loved rock music in general but she was feeling classical music vibes on the road trip.

Soon, Jenna got car sick and her tummy began to hurt. In fact, it started to hurt so badly that they had to stop the car and she took a step out. Unfortunately, after about 5 more minutes she threw up. They got back in the car and Jenna fell asleep with a pillow under her head and a cozy blanket covering her stomach.

A few hours they finally got to San Francisco, but Jenna was still sick and her parents were beginning to get very worried. So, they decided to play safe and go to the doctor to see if Jenna was okay. However, the doctor said that Jenna wasn't sick at all and she just needed rest. Jenna's parents got mad because they knew that she was sick. So, they took Jenna to more and more doctors until she wasn't sick and had begun feeling better.

Ava & Melody Production, LLC.

Chapter 5
"NORMAL DAY"

S oon after Jenna felt better, she started sleeping with her doll. Every night her parents would stare at her until she woke up. One night she woke up to see that her mother was looking right at her. Jenna though it was some sort of challenge not to blink – but when she blinked, her mom went into the closet.

Jenna thought, "Why would she go in there?"

Jenna went to her parents' room because she got scared. When Jenna entered the room, however, she couldn't move.

She saw her mom and dad sleeping peacefully on the bed.

And then realized that she wasn't holding her doll.

Jenna thought that maybe she had dropped her doll during her sleep, but little did she know that this wasn't what had actually happened. Jenna was terrified but she fell asleep on her parents' bed and woke up feeling tired the next morning.

The next morning was Christmas and Jenna was so happy. When she woke up, she smelled the hot coca in the air. Jenna forgot that there was no school for the whole week of Christmas.

Jenna hugged her parents and asked, "What are we having for breakfast today, Mom?"

"We've got gingerbread cookies, banana bread, hot coca, and some warm French toast," said Jenna's mother.

Jenna was starving, so she walked straight over to the small table her parents had put in the hotel room. Her dad was cooking some other meals so they could eat. Jenna acted like she hadn't seen anything the previous night but she couldn't stop thinking about it.

Jenna ate up and thanked her mother and father for the food.

Later that day, Jenna's mother was giving her a haircut. After what felt like a few hours, Jenna showed her father the haircut. Her blonde, silky hair flowed in the air. Her hair was beautiful. Jenna ran to look in her suitcase and picked out a blue striped

Ava & Melody Production, LLC.

dress with flowers on it. She put on the dress and came out to show her parents, but they were busy, so Jenna grabbed her coat and went to leave the hotel. She stood in the hotel lobby for a moment, then put on her black fabric coat and walked outside. When she saw that it was raining, she gave up and went back to the hotel room.

Chapter 6
"THE DOLL"

When Jenna came back inside, the lobby was pitch black. Jenna was sure she could hear voices that kept saying, "I will find you." But about five minutes later, the voices stopped – and she saw her doll in front of her.

Jenna screamed. When she blinked again, she saw that her doll was gone, the lights were on, and everyone in the hotel was looking at her. Some even came up to her to see if she was hurt. When they asked if Jenna was okay, she simply passed out from horror.

Five hours later...

Jenna woke up in the hospital. She had a breathing tube in her mouth and needles inserted in her arm giving her something "cardiostimulatory."

When Jenna woke up, a memory from her past came to her from when she was eight years old and playing with her sister. Her sister had died a couple of years back. Soon after, Jenna's memory faded away.

When Jenna got back to her hotel and was comfortably in her bed, her parents gave her the doll she had chosen. However, when she held the doll she realized that it felt... dense. So, she asked her parents if they had done anything to the doll, but they said they hadn't. Jenna began to get a little concerned about her parents, because they hadn't once asked how she was feeling.

Jenna's father had room service bring them up some strawberry cheesecake, two cups of coffee, mint tea, and a brownie.

Jenna had a sip of her tea and it tasted more minty than ever. Her mother and father had some black coffee and a strawberry cheesecake that shone as brightly as a diamond, with a sweet-looking strawberry on the top. Jenna also had a brownie that tasted like the inside of a chocolate cake, although the top was white and harder. It took a couple of seconds to truly taste the cake.

After eating, Jenna fell asleep, as did her parents.

Jenna woke up the next day to the sound of birds tweeting and the feeling of her arm still hurting from the needles that had been injected into her. Thankfully, Jenna's hotel was also next to an ocean, so Jenna heard the beautiful sound of the bright, blue, glistening waves crashing on the soft ocean sand, making a splash that sounded better every time.

Soon it was time for breakfast. Jenna felt a small amount of sadness because they were leaving in a week.

Today the hotel was serving hashbrowns, sweet pancakes, waffles with maple syrup drizzled on them, extra-crispy bacon, and sizzling sausages next to some stations of milk and chocolate milk. All this made Jenna's mouth drool. Jenna brought her doll with her but she noticed that her doll wasn't dense anymore and, oddly, her parents were normal again.

The last day at the hotel...

It was the last day of being at the hotel and Jenna was so sad, but her dad said to her that he was going to make the same breakfast, lunch, dinner, and dessert that the hotel made.

Those words made Jenna smile. Jenna's mother said that they could get candy from the gas station on the way back. Jenna was even happier, but she was still thinking about the doll.

Ava & Melody Production, LLC.

Chapter 7
"IT'S YOUR FAULT"

When Jenna and her family got in the car, Jenna realized that her mom and dad were acting weird once again. When Jenna looked at them more closely, she saw that their hair was looking a little orange... like her doll's hair.

Jenna was scared, too scared to tell them what was happening.

Jenna looked at her doll and asked, "What is happing? What is happening to my family!?"

But then something happened – something that would make Jenna scream. It started raining and the clouds turned grey. Loud thunder boomed and rain poured.

But then Jenna's doll turned and said, "What did I ever do to you, huh? What did I do to you, Jenna?" The doll's voice got louder, "WHAT DID I DO TO YOU, HUH, JENNA!? WHAT!?"

Jenna started to cry and said, "N-n-nothing! Please leave me alone, please!"

Jenna's parents turned and kept repeating, "It's your fault, it's your fault, it's your fault, it's your fault! It's your fault, it's your fault, it's your fault, it's your fault!"

To be continued...

Ava & Melody Production, LLC.

ABOUT THE AUTHOR

Hello, my readers! My name is Ava Jamaleddin and I'm 10 years old. I started writing in 2nd grade and I won two awards for reading and one for art. I am now in 5th grade. I play piano and have a good taste in music. I'm working on my second book, I love horror, I have good grades, I'm very organized, I care for everyone, and more! This book is a thank you to everyone who helped me through this work. And here's a thank you to all my teachers for helping educate me as a student. It's hard to believe that I'm one year away from being in middle school. My dream is to become a really good writer, because all my life I've had more and more ideas. I can't help it – I always want to write it down on a sheet of paper. I hope you have a spectacular day.

--- AVA JAMALEDDIN